the **BAD GUYS**

GUYS

in

ALIEN vs
BAD GUYS

ALL RIGHTS RESERVED. PUBLISHED BY SCHOLASTIC INC., *PUBLISHERS SINCE 1920*, 557 BROADWAY,
NEW YORK, NY 10012. scholastic AND ASSOCIATED LOGOS ARE TRADEMARKS AND/OR REGISTERED TRADEMARKS
OF SCHOLASTIC INC. THIS EDITION PUBLISHED UNDER LICENSE FROM SCHOLASTIC AUSTRALIA PTY LIMITED.
FIRST PUBLISHED BY SCHOLASTIC AUSTRALIA PTY LIMITED IN 2017.

THE PUBLISHER DOES NOT HAVE ANY CONTROL OVER AND DOES NOT ASSUME ANY
RESPONSIBILITY FOR AUTHOR OR THIRD-PARTY WEBSITES OR THEIR CONTENT.

O PART OF THIS PUBLICATION MAY BE REPRODUCED, STORED IN A RETRIEVAL SYSTEM, OR TRANSMITTED IN ANY
RM OR BY ANY MEANS, ELECTRONIC, MECHANICAL, PHOTOCOPYING, RECORDING, OR OTHERWISE, WITHOUT WRITTEN
RMISSION OF THE PUBLISHER. FOR INFORMATION REGARDING PERMISSION, WRITE TO SCHOLASTIC AUSTRALIA, AN
IMPRINT OF SCHOLASTIC AUSTRALIA PTY LIMITED, 345 PACIFIC HIGHWAY, LINDFIELD NSW 2070 AUSTRALIA.

ISBN 978-1-338-18959-9

10 9 8   19 20 21 22

PRINTED IN THE U.S.A.   23
6TH PRINTING, 2019

• AARON BLABEY •

the BAD GUYS

in

ALIEN vs BAD GUYS

SCHOLASTIC INC.

GOOD GUYS CLUB SAVES THE WORLD

There are celebrations the globe tonight, as th

**DR. RUPER
MARMALAD**

has been **DEFEAT**

TIFFANY FLUFFIT

6

Yes, that's right—every kitten, puppy, bunny, pony, and dolphin has been turned from a

FLESH-EATING ZOMBIE
BACK into our cute and furry friends!

And **WHO** do we have to thank?

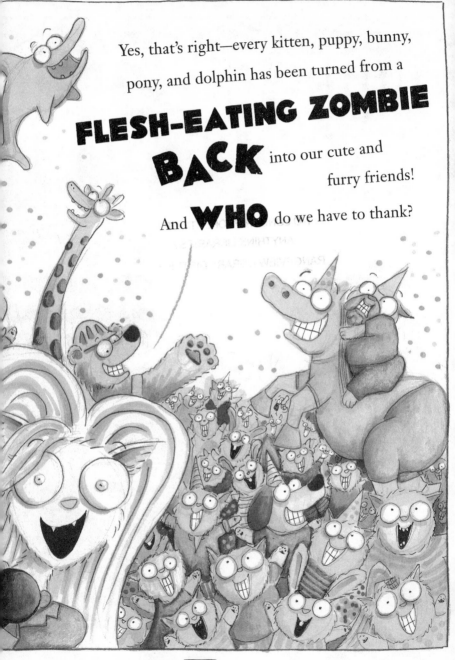

THE GOOD GUYS CLUB!

Sure, the nam
might be lame
but I doubt the
a creature on t
planet that woul
like to give tho

WONDERF
WHOLESOI
BOYS
a hug!

3

The **LOVABLE**
Mr. Wolf!

The **BRILLIANT**
Mr. Snake!

The **POWERFUL**
Mr. Shark!

And
HE OTHER ONE
that is some kind of fish.
Possibly a sardine.

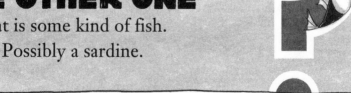

They are the **GREATEST LEGENDS OF OUR TIME!**

ARTIST'S RENDERI.

And I'd personally like to add that I **ALWAYS** thought they were awesome.

I really did . . .

So let's send them all a great, big . . .

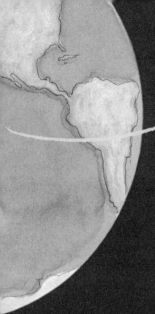

THANK-YOU,

wherever they may be!

To the gang that saved
the world—

NOT BAD, GUYS ...

not bad at all!

It's nice to think of you out there . . .

wherever you are . . .

protecting us . . .

you GREAT, BIG, BEAUTIFUL

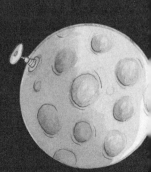

• CHAPTER 1 •
DEEP SPACE, DEEP POOP

think I'm
g to cry . . .

Me too . . .

Pull yourselves together, will you?

WE HAVE TO GET OUT OF HERE!

How?! **HE'S AN ALIEN!**
Marmalade **ISN'T** a guinea pig. Or even the
mad scientist who tried to destroy the world.
He's an enormous hostile alien life-form with

MORE TEETH, TENTACLES,

and **BUTTS** than any decent creature
should have . . .

And we're trapped insid
space station on the mo
**WITHOUT A
ROCKET.**

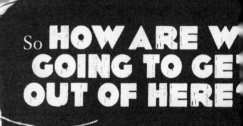

So **HOW ARE W
GOING TO GE
OUT OF HERE**

Shhh! It'll hear us!
What are we going
do? We can't hide
here forever . . .

SPLODGE

Eee...
Nob...
move...

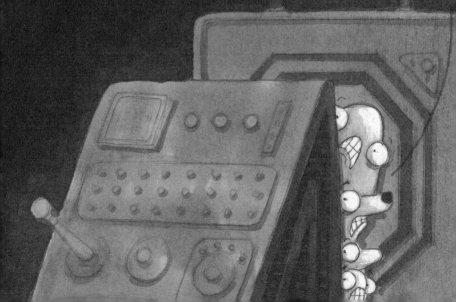

Wait!
It's moving away!
**LOOK AT ALL
THAT GOO!**

SPLODGE!

SPLODGE!

We can't stay here! We have to go!
We have to go! It has too many b

There's just **TOO MANY BUTT**

TOO MANY BUTTS!

Like you can talk,
Mr. Farty-Pants.

Oh man, this is SO not fair.
We've come so far!
Finally, everyone thinks we're
heroes! We can't die here.
We need a plan . . .

Hey! What's *that*?

Legs!
*Where are
you going?!*

SCUTTLE!

SCUTTLE!

SCUTTLE!

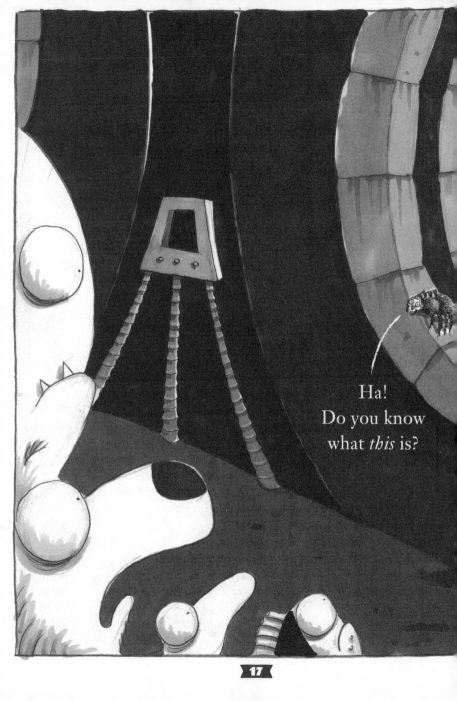

Is it the little room where we all die?

But this is an **ALIEN SPACESHIP!** How will you even know how to work it?

How hard can it be? I bet there are a whole **BUNCH OF LANGUAGES** on here and probably some from **EARTH** and . . . yep . . . what if I just punch in a few **COORDINATES** and . . . yep . . .

I'd say we're good to go!

ready to launch

destination > earth

Man, you just **HACKED AN ALIEN COMPUTER!** Seriously, we don't give you as much credit as you deserve. Let's hear it for Legs, guys!

OK, I'll tell you what— why don't you stay here and **HAVE A PARADE FOR LEGS,** and I'll see you back on Earth. OK?

You are the rudest little—

No, he's right!
EVERYBODY GET IN.
I'll just finish up out here
and we'll be on our way!

· CHAPTER 2 ·
AND THEN THERE WERE FOUR

LEGS?!

Oh no, this isn
good at all . .

Where is he?!

Hey, you
know what?

The ole escape pod is all
GOOD TO GO,
so I say we just jump right
back in and skedaddle,
whaddya say?

Are you serious?

YEAH!

I mean, there are **PLENTY** of these pod things. Legs can just take the **NEXT ONE**.

He's probably just gone to

GRAB A SANDWICH

or something, and I'm sure he wouldn't mind if we took off and met him back on—

NO ONE LEAVE UNTIL WE FIND LEGS. GOT IT?

I mean, yeah, we **COULD** do that, but don't you think it makes more sense to—

WHAT ARE YOU TALKING ABOUT? LEGS IS OUR **FRIEND!** HE'S THE **ONLY REASON** WE KNOW ABOUT THE ESCAPE PODS IN THE FIRST PLACE, AND **YOU WANT TO LEAVE HIM BEHIND?!**

Hey, Piranha! Keep it down!

NO! I'VE HAD IT UP TO HERE WITH THIS ROTTEN LITTLE *DIABLO!*

I'm just **SAYING**, I think Legs would **WANT** us to save—

YOU ARE THE MOST SELFISH . . .

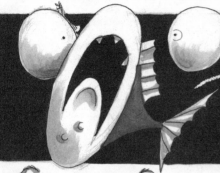

Piranha!

MEAN-HEARTED.

Really, man—*shush!*

SON OF A WORM I'VE EVER.

Is it just me,
or do I have an
ALIEN BUTT
pointed at my face?

Piranha! *Look out!*

PIRANHA!

That's it. I'm out of here.

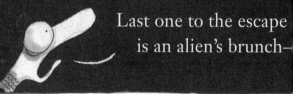

Last one to the escape is an alien's brunch–

Don't even think about it. We have to go after him.

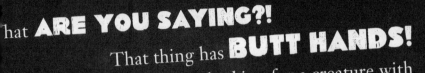

...hat **ARE YOU SAYING?!**

That thing has **BUTT HANDS!**

You really want to go looking for a creature with

great, big, **POOPY**

BUTT HANDS?!

Shut up and listen!

OOOOOOOOOO MAANNNYYYYYY

BUUUUUTTTTTSSSSSSSSS

He's still ALIVE!
We can follow his voice!

Let's

But what about the escape po
Maybe I should stay here an
look after it, just in case . . .

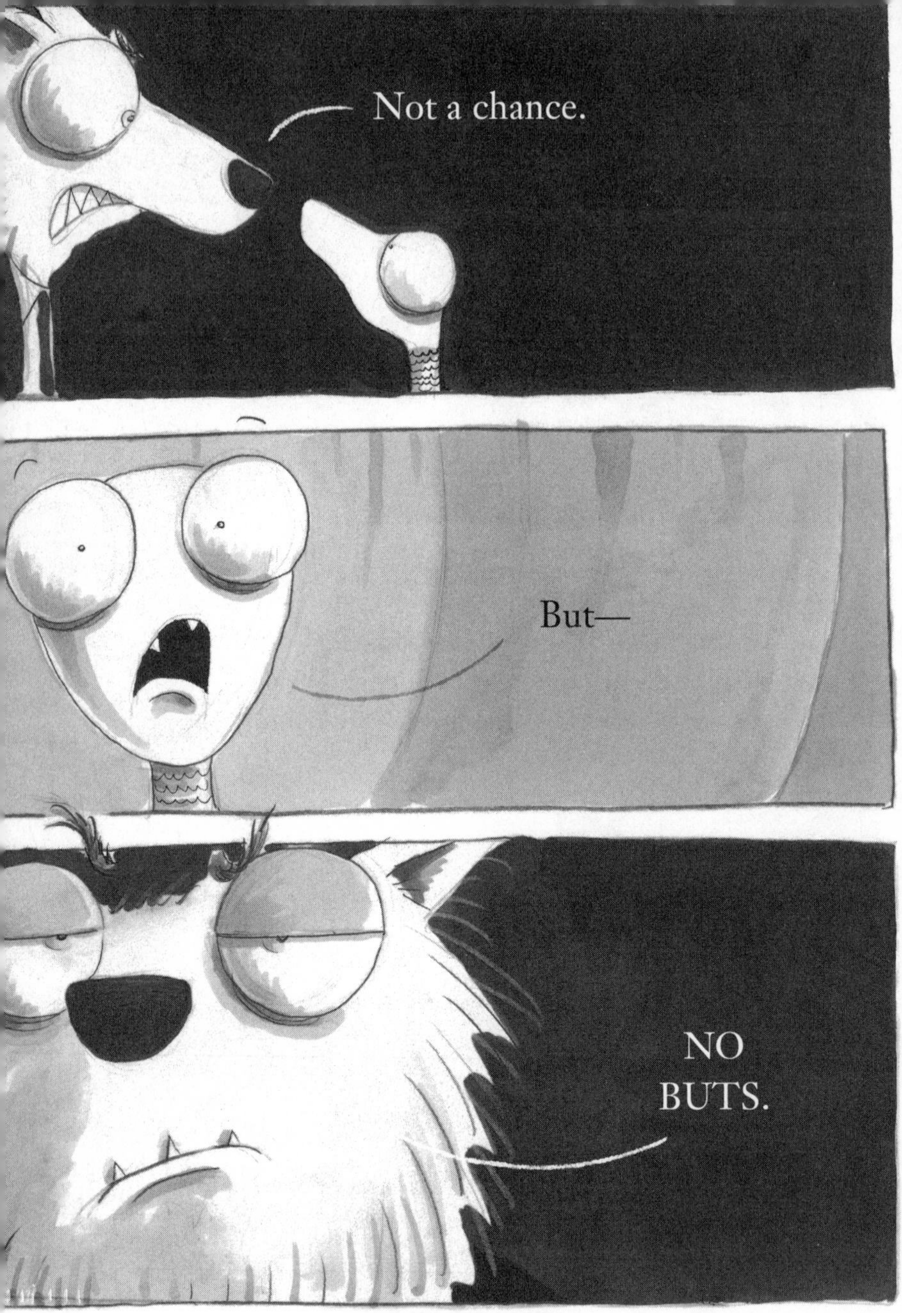
Not a chance.
But—
NO
BUTS.

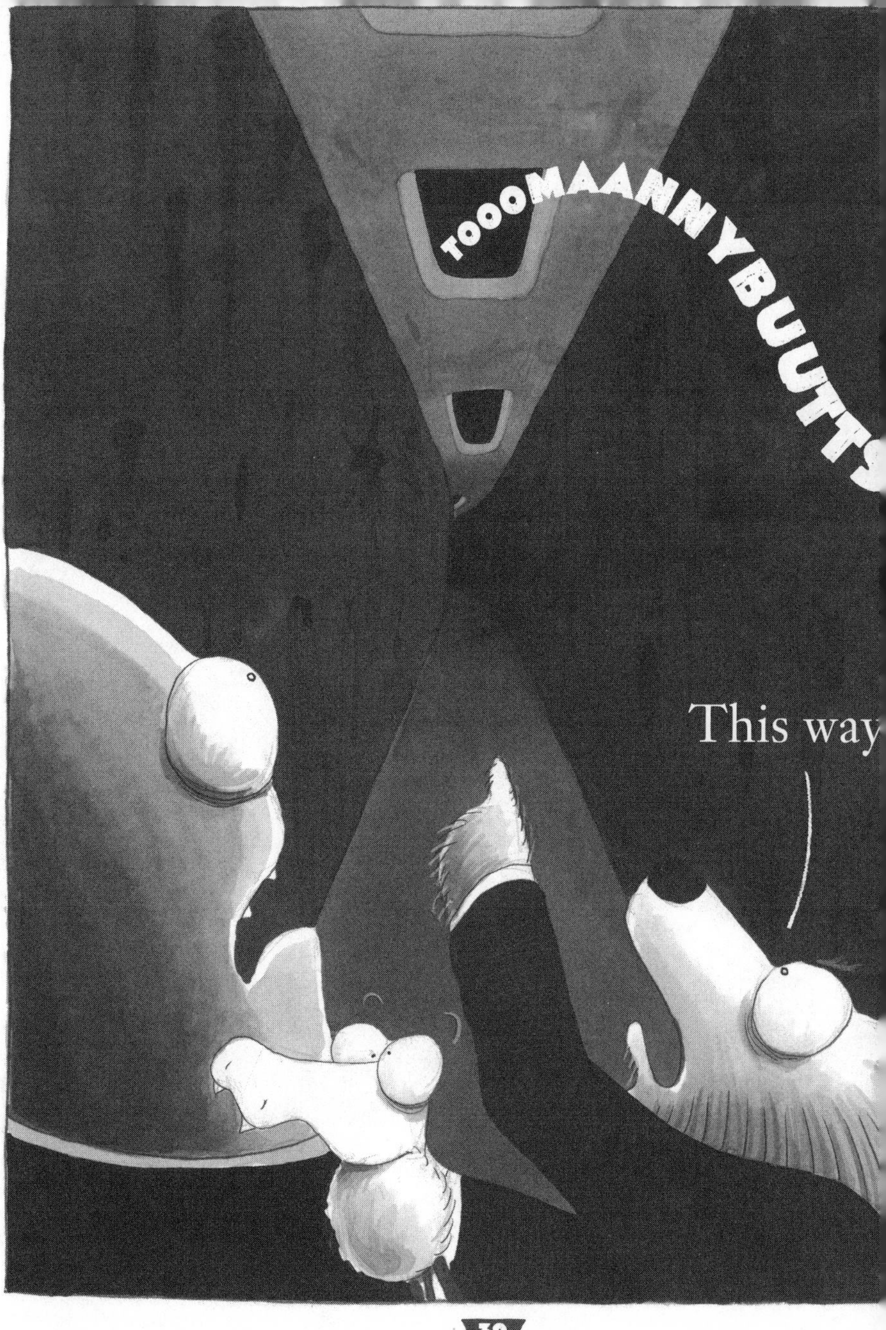
TOOOMAANNYBUTTS
This way

· CHAPTER 3 ·
THE LADY ALIEN

OK, if you vote to stop looking for our friends, raise your hands.

No hands? OK, then, **LET'S KEEP LOOKING!**

Oh, you're hilarious.
I hope the alien takes
you next.

You should be
so lucky—

AAAAARRRGH!
IT'S GOT
ME!

don't like the look of this. These are some

ASTY-LOOKING WEAPONS.

Why does Marmalade . . .
I mean, the *alien* . . . have

O MANY WEAPONS?

This is making me nervous.

Let's get out

of here . . .

No, wait!
Maybe we could use them
AGAINST him!

No, but maybe we could figure it out.

FIGURE IT OUT?!
OK, well, why don't you take a few minutes to learn how to

SPEAK ALIEN

and then flip through the

INSTRUCTION MANUA

and then mosey on over and TEACH US how to use them, too! Ye GREAT idea. Let's just all take a seat a

FIGURE IT OUT!

No! Snake!

Don't interrupt me, mar
You need to hear this—

SNAKE!
IT'S HERE!
AARRGGHH

SHARK?!
Man, you are SO good at disguises.

I know.

But how did you manage to make this so quickly?

I'm just good at it. Let it go.

What's with the **DRESS?!**

I'm going to pretend to be a **LADY ALIEN**. And when the **MARMALADE ALIEN** tries to make friends with me, I'll get him to show us where he keeps the creatures that he's captured and **BINGO—** we can rescue the guys. **THAT'S** the plan.

OK, your disguises may have work
in the past, but what you just saic
is so stupid it makes me want
to eat my own face.

Well, I like it.

IT'S INSANE!

C'mon! His disguises
always work!

Yeah, but this time he's pretending to be a LADY ALIEN and

HE DOESN'T EVEN KNOW WHAT A LADY ALIEN LOOKS LIKE!

That's a chance I'm willing to take.

· CHAPTER 4 ·

AROUND IN CIRCLES

It's so dark.
Why is it so dark?
It seems to be
getting darker . . .
Don't you think it's
REALLY dark?

YES! GREAT OBSERVATION
IT'S DARK! WHAT DO YOU WA
A *COOKIE*?
OBVIOUSLY, IT'S DAR

Give me a break!
I'm **TERRIFIED**!
Everyone's gone. Even Sha
But we can't give up! If we j
keep searching I **KNOW**
we'll find them. We're getti
CLOSE, I can feel it.

Oh really? We're getting *close*
Then how do you explain **THIS**

The escape pods?!
But that means . . .

It **MEANS** we've been **WALKING AROUND IN CIRCLES**.

Listen to me, Wolf . . .

I'll admit it, **PART OF ME** really does want to be a hero. It's true. Part of me really, *really* do

But you know what I've learned from follow

you around on all these stupid missior

Do you know what I've learned fr

every ridiculous situation you'v

put us in?

DO YOU?

61

I've learned I'm *not* a hero.
I know you want me to be one . . .

But I'm really, really not.

I know **YOU** want to be a hero.
And who knows—
MAYBE YOU ARE.
But I also think that you're **CRAZY**.
And I think, one day, you'll make
just one too many stupid decisions
and you **WILL** go and get
yourself eaten by an alien.
And, Wolf?

I think that day is today.

I've never had a friend before, Wolf. And even though I do call you an idiot kind of a lot . . . I know that you're the best friend I'll ever have. And I don't want to lose you. So . . .

Please get in the escape pod with m

You know I can't, Mr. Snake.

And you know why, too.

I can't **MAKE** you do anything, buddy. What you do next is up to you. There's the **ESCAPE POD**. If you really want to leave, then go ahead, get in and go. But I have a feeling that you'll do the right—

WHAT?!

I didn't think you'd actually get in!

Why? Because of my little speech? Well, yeah, I meant it and everything, but there's an

ALIEN WITH BUTT HANDS

out there, so basically,

ALL BETS ARE OFF

and—

What?

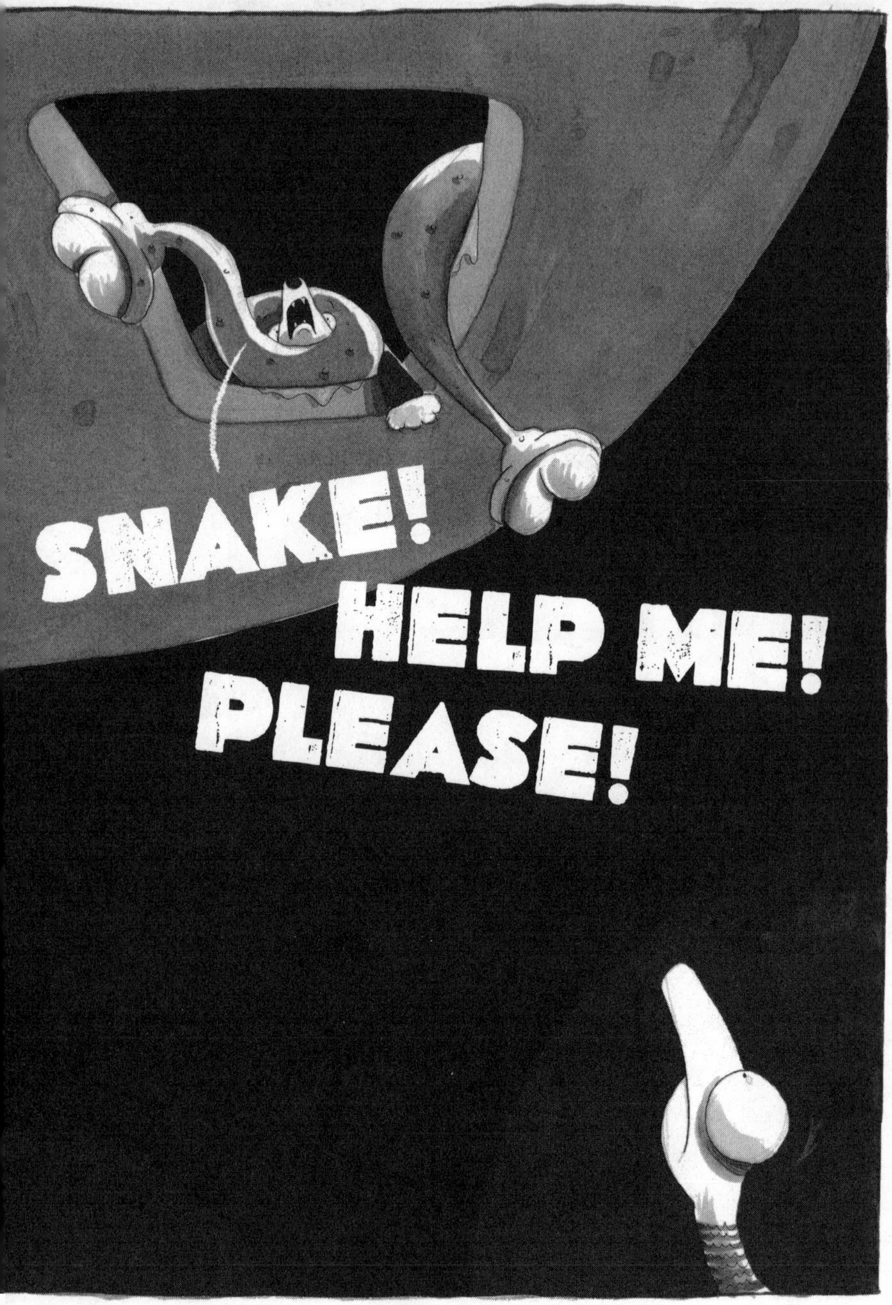
SNAKE!
HELP ME!
PLEASE!

· CHAPTER 5 ·
THE PIT OF DOOM

What **IS** this stu

I can't say for certain,
but I'm pretty sure it's
DRIED ALIEN SNOT,
hermano.

Piranha!

ah, it's **DRIED SNOT**.
came out of the alien's nose holes.

Shark!

Well, considering how
many butts it has, I
suppose we should be
grateful it's just snot.

Legs!

Hey, Wolfie. I've got to be honest—we were kind of hoping next time we saw you, you'd be **RESCUING US**

It's true. We're happy to see you, but I think we're all pretty disappointed, too.

Yep. I don' know wha else to say.

LET ME SHOW YOU...

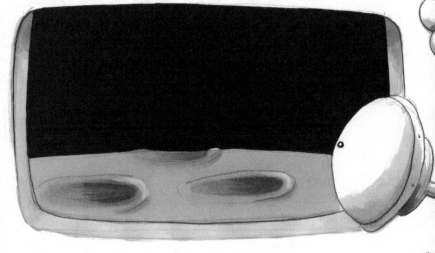

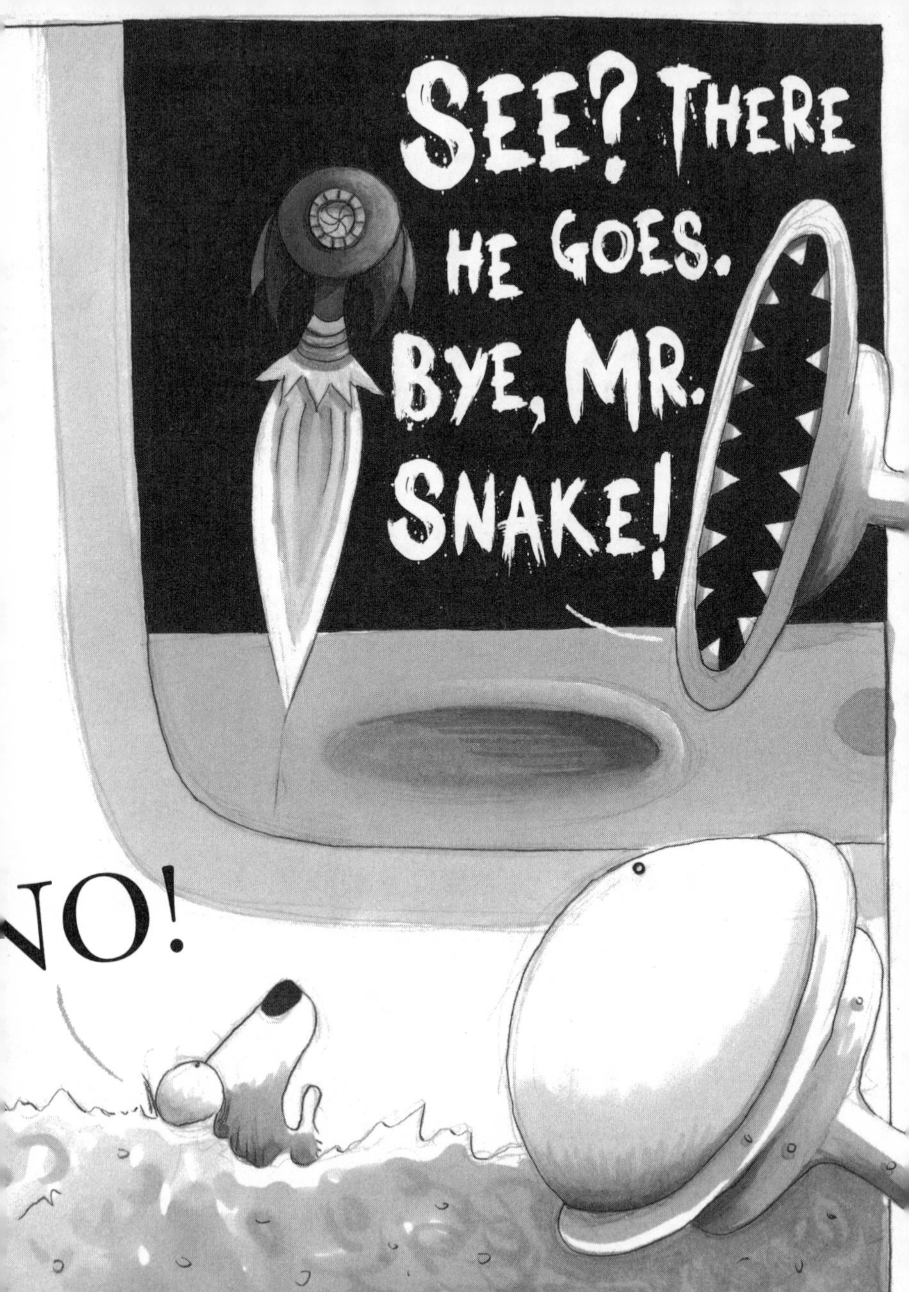
SEE? THERE HE GOES. BYE, MR. SNAKE!
NO!

CHAPTER 6

THE END OF THE ROAD

Hey, you! Butt hands!
When you **FART**,
it from a single tentacle
or do all the disgusting
things go off at once?

WELL, I'M NOT
SURE, LITTLE
FISHY....

LET'S FIND OUT!

Oh man, I didn't think that through . . .

Hey, Marmalade! Wh
did you pretend to be
GUINEA PIG? W
was the point of that

WELL, NO ONE TAKES MUCH NOTICE OF SILLY LITTLE GUINEA PIGS. SO I WAS ABLE TO STUDY YOUR PLANET VERY CAREFULLY WITHOUT ANYBODY NOTICING . . .

And what did you learn?

APART FROM THE FACT THAT PIRANHAS AND SHARKS DON'T NEED TO BE IN WATER AS MUCH AS YOU'D THINK?

Yeah. Apart from th

I LEARNED THAT YOUR PLANET IS HELPLESS.

AND IT WI BE MIN

I feel so stupid. I thought you were doing all of this just because you didn't like being **CUTE** and **CUDDLY**.

OH, THAT WASN'T A LIE. ON MY PLANET, I AM CUTE AND CUDDLY. AND I HATE IT. DON'T GET ME STARTED.

Is your name even Marmalade?

YOU COULDN'T PRONOUNCE MY REAL NAME, WOLF.

HAT DO I WANT WITH **YOU?**
ANT TO **EAT** YOU. BUT NOT
FORE I SHOW YOU THE
ESTRUCTION OF
YOUR PLANET!

Yeah, yeah. That sounds great, KDJFdddd— whatever, and yeah, we all saw your weird, creepy **WEAPONS**, but you know what? You don't stand a chance!

OH REALLY? AND WHY'S THAT?

Because there's only **ONE** of you you're no match for **AGENT F** and the **INTERNATIONAL LEAGUE OF HEROES**

HMMM. THAT F IS VERY CLEVER

BUT GUESS WHA

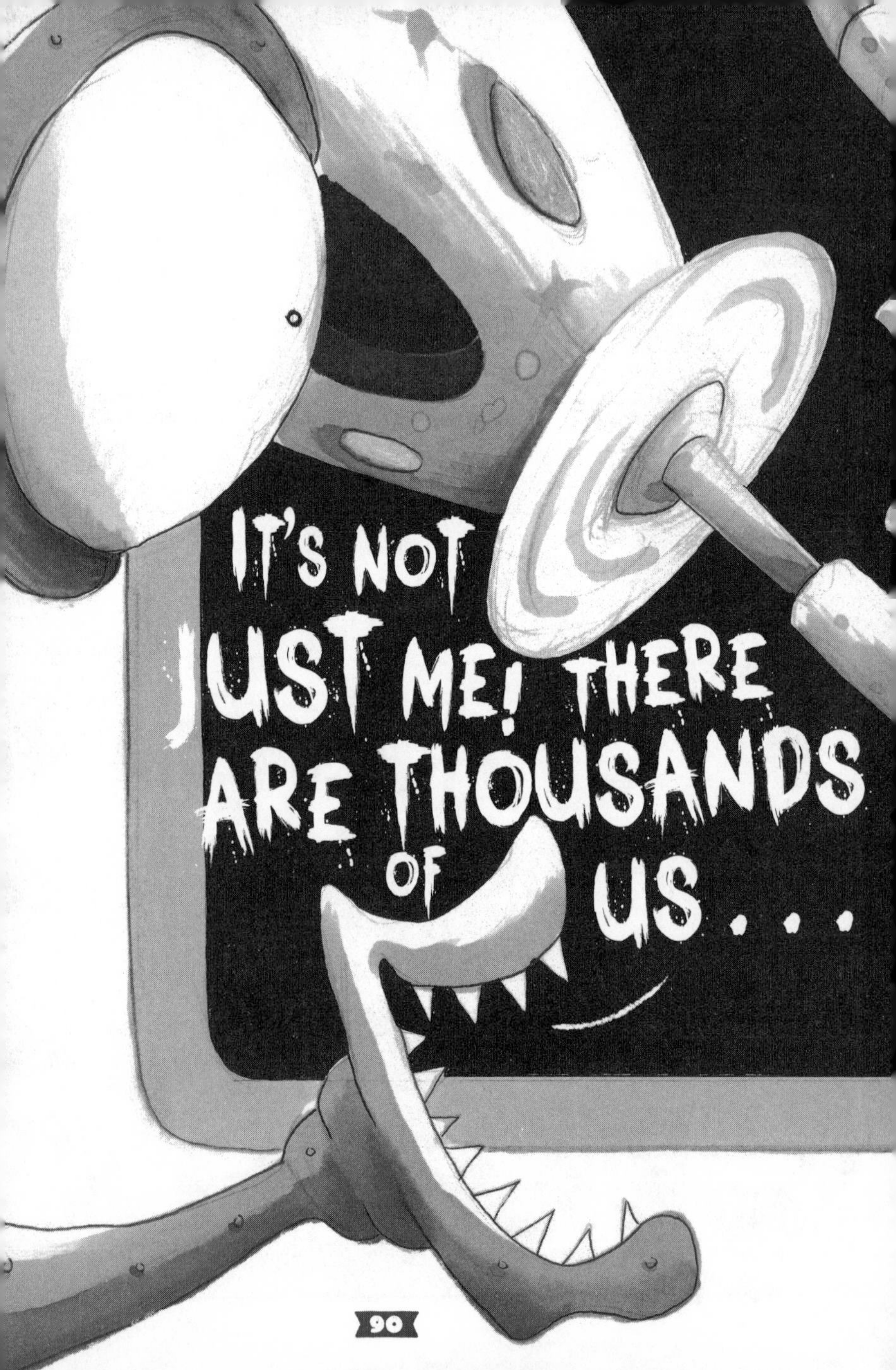
IT'S NOT JUST ME! THERE ARE THOUSANDS OF US . . .

Oh no.

YOUR WORLD IS OURS.

ND YOU KNOW WHAT? I DON'T THINK I WANT TO KEEP YOU AROUND ANY LONGER.

I. SUDDENLY FEEL VERY HUNGRY.

Hey

GET AWAY FROM HIM, YOU BUTT-HANDED MONSTER!

SNAKE!

CHAPTER 7

CK ON SOMEONE
YOUR OWN SIZE

Bring it, guinea pig.

He's beating the alien with his own butts!

EVERYONE HOLD ON TO SOMETHING

DANGER!
OUTER DOOR

CLUN

Hey, malade!

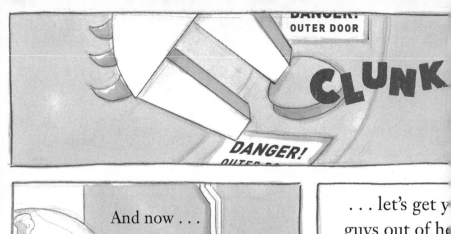

You did it, Snake!

YOU CAME BACK!

**OU CAME
BACK!**

What changed
your mind?

I guess I just finally got sick of being a Bad Guy.

Hey, *chicos*!
As much as I want to dance my dance of joy right now, there's a whole

ALIEN ARMY OUT THERE WAITING TO DESTROY EARTH

We need to get home and warn **AGENT FOX.**

It's **KDJFLOER HGCOINWERU HCGLEIRWFHEK LWJFHXALHW!**

But how?!

MY SPECIES CAN HOLD OUR BREATH IN SPACE FOR UP TO NINE WEEKS, IF WE HAVE TO. SO I JUST FLOATED AROUND TO THE BACK DOOR . . . .

AND
FRIEN
LET N
BACK

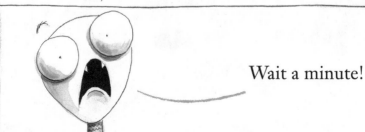

Wait a minute!

· CHAPTER 8 ·
THE POD

TO THE
ESCAPE POD!
HURRY!

I'm sorry, Legs, I had to fire off the first pod to **TRICK** Marmalade. How long will it take you to prep another one?
I'll do it as fast as I can, Mr. Hero!
Snake, I'm so proud of you! I mean . . . *how did you get that weapon thing to work?!*

I just . . . figured it out.

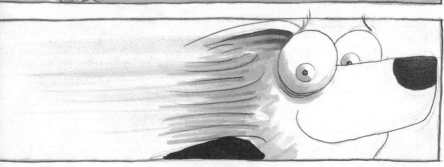

SNAP!

EEEEEE! Oh man, they're everywhere!

Watch out!

That's it! **THE DROOL!** Everyone—GET ON MY BACK!

Now hold on **TIGHT.**

Legs, I hate to rush
you but—

I'm on it . . .

I don't mind rushing you!

HURRY, CHICO!

I'm on it!

Everyone, get in!

Um . . .

Um, *WHAT*?!

There's a setting here that kind of bothers me. I'm not sure what it means.

WHO CARES WHAT IT MEANS?!

JUST GET IN HERE AND SEND US BACK TO EARTH!

Yeah . . . OK . . . I guess it'll be OK . . .

Oh no!
They're
HERE!

CLUNK!

But *we're*
NOT!

• CHAPTER 9 •
UT OF THE FRYING PAN, INTO THE—
NG ON, THAT'S NOT INVENTED YET...

WE'RE HERE!

WE'RE BACK ON EARTH!

Uhhhh . . . yep. We are back on Earth . . .

mission location

I can't lie, *chicos*. I thought there'd be a crowd waiting to welcome us. I've got my party pants on . . .

Yeah. And we have to warn Agent Fox.

Where is everyone?

Maybe we're just in the **WRONG SPOT.**

Did we land in another country or something?

Uhhhh, no. As far as I can tell, we've landed right back where we arranged to **MEET AGENT FOX.**

What do you mean, Legs? We're in the **MIDDLE OF NOWHERE**. You must be reading that thing wrong.

Hmmm. I wish I was . . .

Don't stress, guys! We're home! That's the main thin We're home, but this time it's *different*. This time we' **HEROES!**

Ohhhhh. Being heroes isn't the only thing that's different . . .

What do you mean, Legs?

Well, remember that etting that was bothering me? It seems . . . it was the control for a slightly

DIFFERENT KIND OF TRAVEL . . .

You mean, that's the thing that made us go so **FAST?**

Well, maybe . . . but that's not what I mean . . .

Spit it out, Spider! **WHERE ARE WE?!**

Mr. Snake, the question isn't **"WHERE"** . . .

It's **"WHEN."**

Look!

Dudes . . . I think we **TIME-TRAVELED!**

year > 65,000,000 BC

location > earth

65 MILLION BC?!
Are you kiddin

65 MILLIO
BC?! But that's when

When, what?

Oh my stars!
You're right!
That's when
there were . . .

That's when there were

WHAT?!

TO BE CONTINUED . . .

T'S ON.

...hing can rival the **TERRIFYING** ...r of the **DINOSAURS**. Except ...be **THE BAD GUYS**! This is **WRONG**. This is *all* **BAD**. This **AWESOME**!

Look for a super-sized adventure with
the BAD GUYS *in*
Do-You-Think-He-Saurus?!

With quizzes, games, and more bad-to-the-bone extras!